I0542651

CORNELL DYER AND THE OLD FOLKS HOME

An *Adventures of Cornell Dyer*
supernatural mystery

Denise M. Baran-Unland

In collaboration with
Timothy M. Baran

Illustrated by Sue Midlock

This book is lovingly dedicated to the reader, whoever you might be.

"My wretched passions were acute,
smarting, from my continual, sickly
irritability I had hysterical impulses, with
tears and convulsions" – Fyodor Dostoyevsky

TABLE OF CONTENTS

Prologue

Chapter 1: No More Mysteries

Chapter 2: The Girl at the Five and Dime

Chapter 3: Into the Montage

Chapter 4: Closing Up Shop for the Night

Chapter 5: Roadblock

Chapter 6: The Gate Between the Trees

Chapter 7: When the Sun Goes Down

Chapter 8: Captured!

Chapter 9: Macabre Museum

Chapter 10: A Sugar High That Mustn't Die

Epilogue

PROLOGUE

"Fire!"

The man zoomed through the building screaming the horrible words over and over again. "Fire! Fire!"

Fire!

Amanda's heart nearly stopped.

No, she thought. Not fire!

She ran outside to see. Everyone else ran outside to see.

A crown of red and orange spikes ripped through the fields. Amanda choked on thick black smoke. The rest started coughing.

"No!" the people cried between coughs.

But they could do nothing to stop it, not even Amanda. They could only stand and cough and cry. They could only watch the fire take it all away.

They watched the fire eat their dreams. They watched until the flames burned to sparks, and the smoke shrank to gray wisps.

Then, slowly, very slowly, they unlocked the door and shuffled back inside.

CHAPTER ONE: NO MORE MYSTERIES

"No, Madam! No! Not this week!"

Cornell slammed down the receiver.

The phone in his T-shirt pocket rang. He sighed and pulled it out.

Not again!

"No, Mr. Ardolf! I cannot perform the exorcism on your parakeet until..."

Cornell plopped onto the couch, pulled off his ringing shoe phone, and answered it.

"Mrs. Hullis! I've told you thirty-nine times today! I absolutely cannot find the runaway head to your uncle's ghost until..."

Cornell ripped off his sock phone.

"Mr. Puffin! I cannot rewrap your mummy! Not until,,."

"Mrs. Moore, I can't drain your haunted lake until…"

Enough!

Cornell Dyer grabbed his phone silencing wand from behind the seat cushion and waved it. Instantly he muted all four hundred and sixty-two phones he had scattered around his motor home.

Then he placed an index finger on each temple and willed the radio to tune into his favorite Wagnerian opera.

Cornell had received so many phone calls about lawn ornament covens, vampire cows, haunted trash cans, and werewolves, were cows, were rattlesnakes, and were bed bugs that he was overworked, overtired, underfed, and desperate for a vacation.

Eureka!

He made up his mind then and there.

Cornell Dyer, the world's greatest supernatural super sleuth would take a break from saving the world and take time to pamper himself.

But where should he go? East coast? West Coast? The mountains? The country?

"Hinkledee, pinkledee, wonkedy MOVE!" Cornell cried.

The closet door banged open, and ten folded maps hopped across the room and jumped onto the couch next to Cornell.

One by one, he unfolded them and removed all the brochures he'd stapled to their corners.

Crystal Caves? Nope, too dark, even with the sparkling rocks.

Devil's Island? Nope, because that's where Cornell often expelled supernatural intruders from new homes, which those imps didn't like, not one bit. They'd definitely complain if Cornell showed up. No rest and relaxation!

Wild Unicorn National Park? Nope, too primitive. No motor homes allowed, especially the motor homes of supernatural sleuths. Motor homes disturb the terrain of rainbow poppies, the main food source for the unicorns.

Paradise Falls?

Book a vacation today to Paradise Falls, the most restful, relaxing place in the entire world! Enjoy swimming, boating, and water skiing on Lake Bliss! Build a sandcastle, lounge in the sun, play volleyball, and breathe pure lake air! Every inn features modern amenities, even air conditioning and color television! Stroll up and down Cloud Nine Way with all its gift shops, music shops, movie theaters, and a huge selection of restaurants for your dining pleasure! Everyone smiles at Paradise Falls!

"Hmm," Cornell said as he scratched his ear.

But the weather frog kept nibbling Cornell's ear. Cornell scratched again. Then Cornell froze.

One nibble, followed by a slight pause, and then another nibble, and repeat could only mean one thing.

"Eureka!" Cornell cried again. He gave the weather frog a gentle squeeze. That meant, "Thank you."

The frog croaked, "You're welcome," and hopped to the kitchen.

At that moment, thunder shook the sky. In the next moment, lightening sizzled past his window.

The rainy season had begun at Kangaroo City, Idaho.

He'd do it!

He picked up his phone wand and pointed to a tiny plastic telephone on the bookcase. The phone floated across the room to Cornell and grew big enough to use.

Cornell dialed the number on the brochure.

"Hello, is this Paradise Falls?" Cornell asked. "Please book a room for me. I need a very long vacation."

The next morning, Cornell was on his happy, hurried way to Paradise Falls. He wasn't taking the scenic route. No, the scenic route was far too slow.

Cornell needed a vacation; he was taking a vacation; and he barreled down the road to start that vacation as soon as possible.

Four hours later, Cornell was starving. He saw a diner up ahead. The building was painted white. Its sign had red letters: Flynn's Fresh Fast Food.

The parking lot was full of cars, motorcycles, and trucks. So Cornell had to park his motor home way in the back. Grumbling to himself, he trudged across the parking lot and straight through the door of

Flynn's Fresh Fast Food.

His eyes darted left, right, and right in front of him.

Drat!

The little white diner with the red décor was full of hungry people. Would he find an empty table? Would they eat up all the food? How fast could Flynn serve fresh food?

Really fast, Cornell hoped.

The man with the black and white apron waved at Cornell from behind the cash register. The apron had red letters on the front. The letters said, "Flynn."

"Welcome, friend," the man called. "How may I help you?"

"Are you Flynn?"

"That's right," Flynn said. "I am Flynn, and this is my diner. Please sit anywhere. The menus are on the table."

"Thank you," Cornell said. "I am very hungry, but I cannot stay long."

Cornell found an empty booth in the back. He sat on the squeaky red seat cushion. Then he picked up the sticky menu and read the day's special:

*Cheeseburger Deluxe with Mayonnaise and
Olives
French Fried Onion Rings
Root Beer Float*

"Friend," Flynn called out. "Are you ready to order?"

Cornell turned around. Flynn was at the grill, flipping a burger.

"I'll have the special!" Cornell shouted so Flynn could hear him.

"Coming right up!"

Two minutes later, Flynn set a giant cheeseburger in front of Cornell. He also brought a large platter of crispy onion rings and a giant frosty glass of root beer float.

"Enjoy your fresh fast food," Flynn said with a smile and a wink. He hurried away to cook more fresh fast food.

Cornell bit into the cheeseburger. Hot and juicy.

Cornell nit into an onion ring. Crisp and tender.

Cornell sipped the root beer float: cold, fizzy, and creamy.

Soon Cornell was done eating. He was ready to pay for his food. Just as he stood up, he heard a scream. The scream came from the back of the kitchen.

It was not the scream of a cook who burned his hand.

It was not scream of panic because the diner ran out of toast.

No, it was the scream of a pink Moravian goblin.

Cornell looked at the other customers. They were still eating and talking. They had not heard the scream. He was not surprised.

Only great supernatural super sleuths like himself can hear such creatures. Cornell Dyer was the owner of "The Thaumaturgical World of Professor Cornell Dyer."

He specialized in Amulets, Fortune-Telling (with and without cards), Ghost-Hunting, Horoscopes, Numerology, Palm-Reading, Potions, Séances, Spells, and Vampire-Slaying.

Cornell also specialized in deactivating pink Moravian goblins. These can be very, very, very dangerous to people, especially people in a diner.

But Cornell was on vacation. If Cornell stopped to help, he would miss his vacation.

So Cornell pretended he did not hear

the scream of the pink Moravian goblin. He rushed to the cash register and paid for his food.

"Was everything fast, fresh, and delicious?" Flynn asked, smiling as he rang up Cornell's bill.

"Yes," Cornell said.

Flynn gave Cornell his receipt. "Come back soon."

Cornell ran out the door and didn't stop until he reached the back of the parking lot. Then he, jumped into his motor home and squealed away.

Three more hours later, Cornell saw the sign: Paradise Falls. Painted on the sign was a tanned man on a surfboard and two tanned women playing volleyball.

To Cornell's right was Lake Bliss. To Cornell's left was the woods.

The resort was a paradise all right, he thought.

The downtown area was called Cloud Nine Way. It was a long row of shops. The shops sold everything people needed for a paradise vacation.

As Cornell drove down Cloud Nine

Way, he saw shops that sold beachwear, sandcastle supplies, and suntan oil in three hundred heavenly fragrances.

Cornell also saw restaurants, coffee shops, sandwich shops, beauty parlors, barbers, ice cream shops, candy shops, music shops, and movie theaters.

He drove past an old man with a white beard sitting on a bench outside the Five and Dime. The man was eating caramel corn from a giant paper bag and feeding the pigeons.

The sidewalks were full of young, happy, tanned, energetic vacationers. The warm sunshine made their thick hair shine and their tans glow like gold.

They laughed, and chatted, and poked each other in fun. Some people walked. Some whizzed past on skateboards or roller skates.

Soon he was pulling up to a three-story inn with turrets overlooking Lake Bliss.

The name of the inn was Seventh Heaven. The sign on the roof was shaped like a giant angel. Seventh Heaven inn was as white as foam on a wave. Its shutters and trim were a perfect sky blue.

Cornell sighed happily as he parked his motor home. He stepped onto the ground, stretched his arms, and deeply breathed fresh lake air.

He heard happy shouts of beachcombers as he trudged to the front porch of Seventh Heaven. He paused, shading his eyes against the bright sunlight. He saw the rainbow dots of many bright swimming suits. He heard the rumble of motorboats and squeals of a lively volleyball game.

Cornell ran up the steps. Time to start the vacation!

The clerk behind the desk was a short balding man with graying hair and a clipped mustache. He looked up from his newspaper when Cornell walked up to his desk.

"I'm here for a very long vacation," Cornell said.

The man opened his book. He even had gray in his eyebrows.

His name sign read: Bob Beaton. Next to his name sign was a dish of wrapped candies.

"You are?" Bob Beaton asked.

"I am Professor Cornell Dyer. I am

the world's greatest supernatural super sleuth. I…"

Bob Beaton yawned. He reached down and pulled out a key and gave it to Cornell. The key was shaped like an ice cream cone.

Then Bob Beaton grabbed a piece of candy, unwrapped it, and popped it into his mouth. Cornell liked this place already.

Bob Beaton yawned again. "Room 321." He grabbed another piece of candy.

"Thank you," Cornell said. He reached inside the dish.

Bob Beaton snatched the dish away.

"My candy," Bob Beaton said.

CHAPTER TWO: THE GIRL AT THE FIVE AND DIME

Cornell was having a great vacation.

He slept for eight hours every night. He loved his room. It reminded him of Lake Bliss. The décor was sky blue, sea green, and foamy white.

Each morning, Cornell took his time stretching. He took his time showering and dressing.

Each morning the people who worked at Seventh Heaven washed all his dirty clothes and put them away. They made his bed. They polished and vacuumed.

The first day, they left a piece of wrapped candy for him. It looked just like the wrapped candy in Bob Beaton's candy dish. It was the best candy Cornell ever ate.

The next day, the housekeepers left two pieces. And the day after that, they left three. Then they just left bowlfuls of candy. Cornell felt as if he'd gone to heaven.

Every day Cornell dashed into the waves. He did the back stroke, the breaststroke, the side stroke, the dog paddle, and the dead man's float.

He waterskied on the back of a boat. He rented a motorboat and zoomed up and down Lake Bliss.

Cornell lay under a large beach umbrella, wiggled his toes, and napped.

He built a half mile's worth of sandcastles.

He tried a third of the scents of the Paradise Fall's suntan oil and decided Sun Kissed Sugar Peach was his favorite.

Four times a day Cornell meandered to Cloud Nine Way for food and even more fun.

For breakfast, Cornell ate pancakes at Great Griddle Cakes and More. He ate stuffed omelets at The Good Egg.

For lunch, Cornell worked his way down the menu at One Hundred and One

Sandwich Variations Sandwich Café.

So far, he'd tried the triple decker bacon club sandwich, leftover turkey salad sandwich, grilled cheese and beet sandwich, tuna melts on rye, fruity peanut butter sandwich (with sliced bananas and strawberry jam), French toast and sausage sandwich, and Welsh rarebit with slices of actual rabbit.

For dinner, Cornell walked down Cloud Nine Way and chose a restaurant by playing this game:

> *Bubble gum, bubble gum, in a dish*
> *How many pieces do you wish?*

Then Cornell thought a number to himself and counted. Then he counted restaurants when he walked.

When he came to the number in his mind, Cornell walked inside that restaurant. No one told him to put on a shirt and tie. Swim trunks and sandals were fine.

Paradise Falls was full of rest and relaxation, But Paradise Falls was also full of energy.

Tanned young men with rippling

muscles and tanned young women in bikinis and long flowing hair zoomed past him on skateboards, roller skates, and bicycles.

Cornell heard the "briiing-briing" of bicycle bells and the "cling-cling" of shop bells.

Everybody snacked on candy and ice cream. No one got a tummy ache or a tooth ache.

Upbeat, cheerful music floated out of the shops and into the streets.

Boom bippity boom bippoity lalallala, dut, de dut de dut, lalala, uh, uh, uh…

The sun shone all day. The air was not too hot, not too cold.

Even the cars, sleek with fresh wax, drove slowly down the street. No one was in a hurry. Cornell was not in a hurry either.

Each day after breakfast, Cornell walked to the Five and Dime. An old man or an old woman was always sitting outside. He or she was always eating or drinking something sweet. They were always feeding the pigeons.

Cornell liked the Five and Dime. He

always ordered an orange fountain drink with a scoop of vanilla ice cream on top.

The clerk behind the counter, Charlie Berry, always munched brightly colored candy as he mixed Cornell's drink.

And then Cornell always played checkers. Cornell was very good at checkers. Everyone agreed it was true.

"Wow! Where did you get all your knowledge?"

"What a great checkers player!"

"I'm so...so...stunned!"

Cornell also told stories about the supernatural mysteries he solved

Of course, a great supernatural super sleuth such as he never, ever gave up his secrets. But Cornell could, and did, share stories of his exploits.

Cornell told them how he found a missing tombstone, broke a curse, and recovered Viking treasure at Cap Crag Maine.

Cornell told them how he learned the secret behind a necklace that stole people's memories.

Cornell told them how he crossed an eerie lake. Others had tried crossing before

Cornell, but they never returned.

Cornell told them how he captured never robbers and time traveled.

Cornell told them how he came to the brink of death and back again.

Cornell told them how he slayed vampires, banished ghosts, snuffed out poltergeists, and unwrapped the most sinister plans of mummies.

Each time Cornell told a story, everyone "oohed" and "ahhed."

They gasped and clapped and drooled.

He dried up the ink of many pens with requests for his autograph.

This was most work Cornell hoped to do on this vacation.

One morning on his way to the Five and Dime, Cornell passed an old man feeding the pigeons. This man wore a wide-brimmed hat. He was eating a giant chocolate bar.

Cornell heard "oohing" and "ahhing" from inside. He heard gasping and clapping and drooling. He hurried through the door.

A crowd circled a young woman.

The woman wore a blue shirt with a pocket and a patchwork midi skirt. Bangles dangled from her ears and her neck. Bangles jangled around her wrists.

A brown fedora topped her head. Her bronze curls jounced off her shoulders as she waved her hands.

"What happened next?" one man gasped.

She tossed her head. "Ha! No pink Moravian goblin is a match for a supernatural super sleuth. I told Flynn that I..."

"Madam!" Cornell shouted. "Who are you?"

She whirled around. She put her hands on her hips and looked him up and down. She smirked.

Then she tossed her head again.

"My name is Professor Christine Lucille BeckmanShire. I am the world's greatest supernatural super sleuth the world has ever seen. I specialize in Amulets, Fortune-Telling (with and without cards), Ghost-Hunting, Horoscopes, Numerology, Palm-Reading, Potions, Séances, Spells, and Vampire-Slaying. And I just recently deactivated a certain pink Moravian goblin at..."

"...Flynn's Fresh Fast Food," Cornell

interrupted.

Christine grinned. "Yep. The pink Moravian goblin that you failed to deactivate."

Everyone in the Five and Dime ooohed.

"Madam, I, Professor Cornell Dyer, I and no one else, is the world's greatest supernatural sleuth the world has ever..."

Christine yawned. "Blah, blah, blah. You couldn't even deactivate a little baby pink..."

Everyone at the Five and Dime aahed.

Cornell was really mad now!

"Miss BeckmanShire, supernatural sleuths on vacation don't waste their time..."

Christine blew on her nails. "Huh. I didn't waste my time. I muttered a few magic words while I read the menu."

Everyone at the Five and Dime gasped.

Christine held out her hand. As if by magic, Cornell's hand moved to Christine's hand and shook it.

Everyone at the Five and Dime clapped.

"Come on," Christine said. "I'll buy you a drink. What'll ya have? The orange fountain drink with a scoop of ice cream is tops."

Cornell glared and pointed his finger at the other customers. "Don't you dare drool!"

"Two orange crushies deluxe, please, Charlie," Christine called out to the clerk.

"Coming right up, Professor," Charlie said. He grabbed a handful of candy.

Christine opened her coin purse and paid for the drinks. Then she slid into the back booth.

"Over here, Cornell!" she called. "You should see my motor home. I have a sonic space traveler 53 engine! It's parked by Happiness Hotel. I'm staying there on vacation."

Cornell sat across from her. "That's 'professor' to you. And my motor home has two sonic space 53 engines."

Christine pursed her lips. "If I call you "professor,' then you'll have to call me, 'professor.' Isn't that silly? Let's just call each other "Christine' and Cornell.'"

Cornell nodded "yes." He didn't know why. Charlie set down their drinks.

"Besides," Christine said with a wink. "I don't need two sonic space traveler 53 engines. I have the model from the twenty-second century. Two are such a waste."

Christine took sip, her eyes dancing and on Cornell. He noticed the charms on her necklace.

She noticed him noticing and grinned again.

"Souvenirs from all the supernatural mysteries I've solved – like the case of the screaming pancake."

"Well, I solved the case of the screaming pancake house! And my megasonic nixie finder can tease any elusive nixie out of any shopper's purse, no matter how well hidden. So there!"

Christine set her hand on top of Cornell's hand. She smiled brightly.

"I like you," she said softly. "I like you, Cornell Dyer."

Cornell glanced at their empty glasses. He twisted toward the counter and called, "Two more orange crushies deluxe!"

They sat all morning and told stories of the mysteries they'd solved.

They had lunch at the One Hundred and One Sandwich Variations Sandwich Café and ordered the first sandwich on the menu.

Later they ordered the second.

And then the third. And the fourth.

They never made it to the beach that day.

They didn't notice when the sun sank, and the crowds went home

For their conversation remained as fresh and exciting as the first words they had spoken to each other.

CHAPTER THREE: INTO THE MONTAGE

Cornell started each dreamy morning with the sparkle in Christine's eyes.

He ended drowsy nights with the smile on her face.

They watched the sun rise and the sun set.

Hand in hand, they ran through rolling waves.

They joined lively volleyball game and won, with everyone cheering for them.

They bought a red, yellow, and blue-striped beach ball. They took turns inflating it. They tossed it back and forth, never minding the spray from the waves.

They built a sandcastle, which became a sand neighborhood, which became a sand city. SNAP! SNAP! SNAP went the cameras of all the smiling people on the beach.

They shared a double-checker ice cream waffle cone, a wand of cotton candy, a foot-long chili cheese dog, and wads of pink bubblegum.

They walked along the empty beach at sunset, kicking cool sand over each other's feet.

They sprinted across the crowded beach at noon, dodging sunbathers, laughing, and squirting each other with squirt guns.

They sneaked through the side doors of the movie theaters after lunch. They watched old monster flicks in the cool dark and fed each other popcorn.

They ordered double portions of surf and turf at candlelight dinners. They ate from the other's plate.

They propped an easel on the sidewalk and tackled the same paint-by-number landscape. They admired each other's progress and ignored any crossing of lines.

They roller-skated, skate-boarded, and bicycled along Cloud Nine Way.

They tried the other one-hundred and fifty varieties of suntan lotion. They took turns rubbing rubbed scented oil into each other's backs.

They swapped stories at the Five and Dime. Everyone "oohed" and "ahhed" and gasped and clapped and drooled. And they dried up the ink of many pens by signing so many autographs.

They crowded beneath a single beach umbrella and took turns reading aloud. They read their favorite detective stories by Edgar Allan Poe and Sir Arthur Conan Doyle.

They swung on the swings, slid down the slides, and raced each other to the top of monkey bars.

They packed picnic meals and colored in coloring books by day.

They gathered sticks and roasted hot dogs over campfires on the empty beach by night.

They wrote anagrams and words lists from their names: Cornell and Christine.

And they both ate plenty of candy.

One night as Cornell walked up the

stairs to Room 321, a phone rang from an inside blazer pocket.

But which pocket? Cornell had lots of hidden pockets.

The phone rang and rang and rang.

Cornell pulled out old mayonnaise packets.

He pulled out a pair of dice.

He pulled out a rotting set of vampire teeth.

He pulled out a werewolf fang.

He pulled out the melted remains of a chocolate bar with almonds.

He pulled out a purple rabbit's foot.

He finally pulled out an old belt buckle, which he answered on the thirty-second ring.

"Professor Dyer!" the woman scolded him. "When are you getting rid of the haunted lake in my back yard!"

Not again!

"Mrs. Moore!" Cornell lost his temper. "I told you last week! I'm taking a few days off to.."

"Last week! Last week!" she screeched. "It's been seven weeks! Get over here right..."

Seven weeks?

Seven weeks?

HOW???

Cornell turned off the buckle phone. He slid it into a random pocket.

"Ouch!"

A gerbil poked its head out.

"You idiot!" the gerbil squeaked, rubbing a tiny paw on its head. "Watch what you're do…"

Cornell stuffed the protesting gerbil back in the pocket.

Seven weeks?

Really, it had only felt like a couple of days.

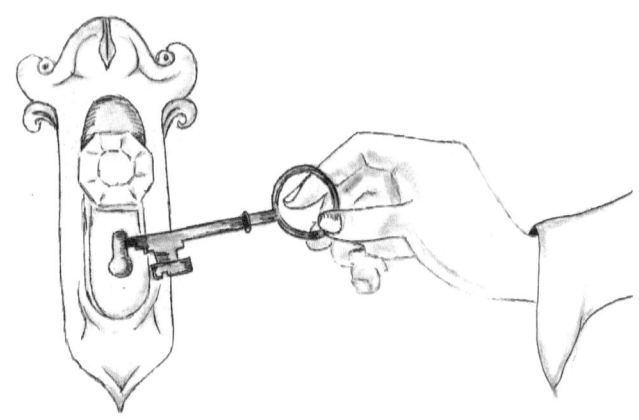

CHAPTER FOUR: CLOSING UP SHOP FOR THE NIGHT

Cornell needed to think. He decided to take a walk.

So he walked back down all three flights of stairs. The lobby was dark and quiet. Bob Beaton was not at his post. His candy dish was empty.

Cornell crossed the room and looked out the window. The waves sloshed. The beach was empty. The inn was too quiet.

Was he the only guest?

He walked outside and through the gardens. He walked all the way to Cloud Nine Way. The entire street was empty. All the buildings were dark.

Very strange, Cornell thought.

Cornell roamed up and down the sidewalks. He peered through darkened windows. It was the same everywhere.

The shops that sold beachwear, sandcastle supplies, and suntan oil in three hundred different heavenly fragrances were all shut up.

The restaurants, coffee shops, sandwich shops, beauty parlors, barbers, ice cream shops, candy shops, music shops, and movie theaters were also closed.

Why would a vacation place shut down when the sun went down?

He strolled back to Seventh Heaven, thinking as he walked. When he got inside, Cornell had an idea. So he went behind the desk and grabbed a handful of keys.

Then Cornell headed down the hall. He held up a key. Its key tag said "107." When Cornell reached Room 107, he slid the key into the keyhole.

The lock clicked. Cornell turned the knob and opened the door.

It's a good thing Cornell didn't take a step. If he had, Cornell might have broken his nose.

The door to Room 107 led to a brick wall.

It was the same with every key Cornell tried. The rooms led to brick walls or empty closets.

But, why?

As Cornell was relocking the Room 300, the floor creaked. Cornell held his breath...and heard breathing that wasn't his.

Cornell whirled around.

Christine!

"What is going on?" she whispered.

"What do you mean?" Cornell stalled.

"I mean," she continued whispering, "every room at Happiness Hotel is fake!"

"Same here," Cornell whispered back. "I walked into town, too. Not a single person..."

"...is in sight and all the shops are closed up," Christine interrupted. "I know. I went over there, too."

Then Christine grinned. "Seems like we've got a supernatural mystery to solve."

We don't have a mystery to solve, Cornell thought. **I** have a mystery to solve.

"It's a mystery," Cornell agreed. "But it might not be a supernatural mystery." He stretched and yawned. "Figure it out if you want. I'm going to bed."

Christine playfully socked his arm. "Me, too. Can't solve mysteries without sleep. Good night, Cornell."

Cornell trudged back to Room 321 and turned on the television. Then he plopped onto the bed and kicked off his shoes.

Humph!

He didn't need any partner to solve a mystery, supernatural or not.

He was Cornell Dyer, the world's greatest supernatural super sleuth.

He specialized in Amulets, Fortune-Telling (with and without cards), Ghost-Hunting, Horoscopes, Numerology, Palm-Reading, Potions, Séances, Spells, and Vampire-Slaying.

And he would solve the Mystery of Paradise Falls all by himself.

That decided, Cornell fell promptly and deeply asleep.

CHAPTER FIVE: ROADBLOCK

The next morning, Cornell woke up with the cheeping of the piping plovers. He was ready to solve the mystery.

He stood at the window and looked at the beach. It was a sunny yellow and full birds and sunbathers.

Cornell was tempted to join them. After all, he was on vacation.

But the mystery nagged at him. So did the memory of not deactivating the pink Moravian goblin.

Today he must be Professor Cornell Dyer, supernatural super sleuth.

Tomorrow he'd be Cornell Dyer, beach bum.

Cornell picked up his key and locked Room 321 behind him.

First stop: breakfast.

Cornell did not meet anyone in the hallway or on the staircase.

Bob Beaton was working the front desk. He was unwrapping a piece of candy from his overflowing candy dish.

Bob Beaton looked up as Cornell passed him.

"Good morning, Professor," Bob Beaton said. "Did you sleep well?"

"Yes," Cornell said. "I always sleep well at Seventh Hea…"

The gray in Bob Beaton's hair and eyebrows was gone. Both were now coal black.

Cornell peered closer. No sign of hair dye.

"Glad to hear it," Bob Beaton said. He grabbed more candy.

Cornell was starving. He wanted a piece of candy, too. All the candy dishes in his room were empty.

But he would not ask Bob Beaton for a piece. Cornell remembered what happened the first day.

So a very hungry Cornell plodded to his motor home. He went inside for the first time in seven weeks.

He found an unopened box of powdered sugar doughnuts. He took a large orange drink out of the refrigerator.

Munching and slurping, Cornell headed to Cloud Nine Way. The shopkeepers had opened their doors and raised their shades.

Tanned young men with rippling muscles and tanned young women in bikinis and long flowing hair zoomed past him on skateboards, roller skates, and bicycles.

Cornell heard the "briiing-briing" of bicycle bells and the "cling-cling" of shop bells.

People walked; people ran.

Everybody snacked on candy and ice cream. Upbeat, cheerful music floated out of the shops and into the streets.

Boom bippity boom bippoity lalallala, dut, de dut de dut, lalala, uh, uh, uh...

The cars, sleek with fresh wax, drove slowly down the street. No one was in a hurry.

On his way into the Five and Dime, Cornell passed an old man in a faded purple tank top. The old man was slurping a chocolate milkshake and feeding the pigeons.

Cornell walked up to the counter and held up his index finger.

Two tanned young men sitting across the room in white T-shirts and shorts saw Cornell walk in. They began setting up the checkers board

"One orange crushie deluxe," Cornell said to the clerk.

Charlie munched from a bowl of brightly colored candy as he mixed Cornell's drink.

The candy looked delicious, but Cornell knew better than to ask.

Or did he?

Cornell reached into the bowl.

Charlie whisked the bowl away. "Mine!"

Very strange, Cornell thought.

Charlie handed Cornell his orange crushie deluxe. Cornell needed to walk and think.

So Cornell turned to the young men.

"Gentlemen," Cornell said. "I cannot play checkers today. I am taking a nice long walk into the woods."

A hush ran through the Five and Dime.

People sipping drinks at the tables stopped sipping.

Feet shuffled.

Everyone looked at everyone else, and then they looked away.

Charlie cleared his throat. He wiped his hands on his apron.

"Um, Professor, I have a problem," Charlie said. "I cannot make your drink. The machine is clogged. Do you have a magical tool to unclog it?"

Cornell must have an orange crushie deluxe. He couldn't walk in the woods if he was thirsty.

"Of course." Cornell reached into his blazer. "I have a number seven socket rocket right here."

"Great!" Charlie said. He lifted up the counter so Cornell could get to the machine. "This is a big help."

The minute Cornell started working, Charlie took off his apron.

"Professor, I will be right back," Charlie said. "I have to make a phone call."

The machine didn't seem clogged to

Cornell. But he did have the right tool to fix it. Soon the orange drink was flowing.

Charlie came back and mixed Cornell's orange crushie deluxe.

"On the house today," Charlie waved Cornell's quarter away. "Thank you for fixing my machine."

Cornell walked out of the Five and Dime, slurping his drink. He headed straight for the road that led to the woods.

But he did not get very far.

A row of bright orange cones blocked the way to the woods. Two tanned men stopped Cornell.

"Professor," one man said. "The road is closed today for construction."

Cornell looked forward and backward. He looked left and right. He did not see any work trucks.

"The trucks will be here soon," the man said. "We're very sorry. But you cannot take a walk in the woods today."

"The beach is still open," the second man said. "The beach is much nicer than the woods."

Both men looked at each other. Then they smiled and nodded at Cornell.

So Cornell turned around and trudged back to Cloud Nine Way. He sipped and scowled and thought grumpy thoughts.

The old man in the purple tank top was now drinking a strawberry one milkshake. He was still feeding the pigeons.

Cornell did not hear the rumble of trucks. So he turned around. He shielded his eyes and looked at the road to the woods. He did not see a truck, not a single one.

So Cornell walked inside the Five and Dime. All the customers stopped talking. They stopped sipping, eating, and playing checkers.

Cornell ordered a second orange crushie deluxe.

"That was a fast walk," Charlie said. He grabbed a handful of candy and mixed Cornell's drink.

"I did not walk to the woods," Cornell said.

Charlie plopped vanilla ice cream into Cornell's drink.

"The road was blocked," Cornell said.

"Oh, dear," Charlie said, shaking his head and clicking his tongue. "Oh, dear. Oh dear."

Cornell's inner sleuthing antenna went up. "Is something wrong?"

Charlie handed Cornell his drink. "I'm sorry you missed your walk in the woods. Enjoy your drink!"

"Thank you," Cornell said.

All eyes stayed on Cornell as he walked out of the Five and Dime.

As he strolled to Seventh Heaven, he did not see any passersby watching him.

But he felt their stares just the same.

CHAPTER SIX: THE GATE BETWEEN THE TREES

Cornell avoided Christine.

He stayed off the beach.

He didn't answer her phone calls on all of his phones in all of his pockets.

He pretended she wasn't knocking at his door.

All day Cornell stayed inside Room 321. He watched television, ate candy, and thought very hard.

The next morning, Cornell woke up at dawn. He ate breakfast in his motor home. Then he strolled to Cloud Nine Away. Way up ahead, he saw the workmen setting up the orange cones.

Fine, Cornell thought. Fine.

He passed an old man in a short-sleeved plaid shirt. The man was licking a triple decker ice cream and feeding the pigeons.

Cornell walked into the Five and Dime.

After ordering an orange crushie deluxe, Cornell went back outside. He sat on the bench next to the old man in the plaid shirt.

Slowly, the man turned to him. His tongue angrily licked the cone. He narrowed his eyes.

"Good sir," Cornell said. "What's wrong?"

The man pointed a gnarled finger at Cornell.

"You," the man growled. "It's my turn to sit in the sun."

Cornell glanced up. Sure enough, the sun was directly overhead.

"No it isn't," Cornell argued. "It's my

turn."

The man's face sagged. Cornell thought he was going to cry.

"Oh," the man said. "I forgot."

The old man stood up and shuffled away, looking over his shoulder at Cornell.

Very strange, Cornell thought.

Cornell sipped his orange crushie deluxe. He tossed sugar-coated breadcrumbs to the pigeons from the bag the old man had left.

He pretended not to watch the old man walking away. But in reality, Cornell was watching him very carefully.

From time to time, the old man turned to see if Cornell was watching him.

When the man came to the orange cones, the two men moved them away. The old man limped into the woods. Then the men blocked the road again with the cones.

Cornell sipped and thought. He must get into the woods.

But how?

Eureka!

Cornell gulped the rest of his orange crushie and then skipped to his motor home.

He rummaged through his costume

closet. He removed only the most important items from his patchwork blazer. Then he stuffed them into the pockets of his jeans.

"Sorry, feller," Cornell told the gerbil.

He hated leaving the gerbil in the motor home. The gerbil was a great lookout. But Cornell was on a dangerous mission, too dangerous for a gerbil.

The gerbil stuck out his tongue and scampered under the couch.

For the next hour, Cornell applied makeup and white hair dye. When he finished, Cornell admired himself in the mirror.

"Hello, Gramps," he said.

Then Cornell sprinkled himself with a short-acting "invisible" powder. He grabbed a magic cane and flew to Cloud Nine Way.

Cornell floated above the walkers, cyclers, skaters, and skateboarders. At the end of the sidewalk, Cornell drifted down. He reversed the powder so the workmen could see him.

The men were still guarding the cones. No work trucks were near the road. No work was being done on the road. The road to the woods looked the same as always.

The men saw Cornell limping up to them.

They smiled at him.

Cornell smiled, too.

They waved, "Hi" to him.

Cornell waved a crooked hand back.

Then they moved the cones aside to let Cornell pass.

Cornell waved a crooked hand in thanks.

And then Cornell hobbled his way along the road that led deep into the woods.

The road was a long, twisty road up a steep hill. Cornell walked and walked for a very long time. His heavy makeup and costume was hot. His throat was very dry.

Cornell wished he'd bought two orange crushies deluxe. But he could not do that. He did not want Charlie, or anyone inside the Five and Dime, to know he was invisible.

Cornell was a very experienced supernatural super sleuth. Cornell had a mystery to solve. Cornell had to remain under wraps.

At dusk, Cornell saw a gap in the trees at the top of the hill.

Beyond the gap was a tall wrought iron

fence. As Cornell neared the fence, he noticed a sign on the gate.

The sign read:

Pinecrest Retirement Community for the Delicately Aged

Cornell peered through the fence. He saw a three-story red brick building.

It should be easy to get in, Cornell thought. I already look delicately aged.

He wondered why Paradise Falls was so secretive about its old folks home. Every city had old folks who needed homes.

Stupid, Cornell thought.

Cornell tried the gate. It was locked. So he reached in his jeans pocket for his skeleton key.

Leaves crunched behind him.

A strong hand clamped around his neck.

A gruff voice said, "What are you're doing?"

Cornell broke free. He whirled around.

It was Christine, grinning.

CHAPTER SEVEN: WHEN THE SUN GOES DOWN

"You!" Cornell cried. "How did you slip past those men?"

For Christine looked like herself.

She wore a blue shirt with a pocket and patchwork midi skirt. Bangles dangled from her ears around her neck and jangled around her wrists. A brown fedora topped her head.

Her bronze curls jounced off her shoulders as she tossed her head and laughed with glee.

She had a backpack slung across her shoulders.

"I'm a girl, silly." Christine flipped her

hair. "Boy, you should have seen your face when I grabbed you. What a scaredy cat!"

"Madam," Cornell retorted. "I am not a scaredy cat. I was thinking very, very hard. You are not scary. You are rude."

"Ha! You look like four scaredy cats."

She pointed to the tiny cuckoo clock on her charm bracelet. "I can call for a ride and get you out of here."

Christine laughed again.

Cornell scowled. She was not one bit funny.

"Step aside," Cornell said. He pulled out his plastic skeleton. "I am unlocking this door and doing some sleuthing."

Christine dug into her skirt pocket and then pulled out two plastic skeletons, twice as long.

"Hey, Cornell, I've got some, too. First one to the lock is the best super sleuth ever!"

Cornell shoved her aside. "Move out of my…"

Christine covered his mouth and dragged him into the bush.

"Hush!" she whispered. "Do you here that?"

Cornell peeled off her hand. He strained to hear.

Swish, swish, swish, swish...

Cornell and Christine listened to the swishing. It was faint, at first.

As they listened, it grew softly louder.

And closer.

Cornell heard other sounds, too.

Mutterings.

And moanings.

And groanings.

And mumblings.

And the heaving of deep, exhausted breaths.

Cornell and Christine peeked through the bush to see what was making the sounds.

It was a very long line of people.

Very, very, very old people with hollow eyes and hanging jaws.

Miles of them.

They slowly dragged their old, tanned, wrinkled bodies up the hill.

And they carried things with them.

Things like beach balls.

And volleyballs.

And buckets and pails for sandcastles.

And roller skates.

And skateboards.

And swimming flippers.

And cages full of shriveled pigeons.

The very last two old people in the line carried the orange cones.

"Cornell," Christine whispered excitedly. "It's everyone from Paradise Falls."

"Shhh," Cornell warned.

The first man in line pulled a chain near the gate. A bell sounded from far away.

While they waited, the old people sagged, arms drooping and talked in tired voices.

"How's the rheumatism, Ethel?"

"Can't make it without two naps anymore."

"Ran out of candy again today."

Everyone made ghostly wails.

Finally the door of the Pinecrest Retirement Community for the Delicately Aged opened. The man in the plaid shirt whose bench Cornell had taken limped out.

The crowed at the gate muttered,

moaned, groaned, and mumbled.

"Hurry up, Jacob," one man snarled.

Jacob pulled out a plastic skeleton from his pocket. He unlocked the lock. He slowly opened the heavy door.

The door creaked as it swung back.

One by one, they shuffled through the gate, hundreds of them.

Then Jacob moved the creaking gate back into place with a loud clang. He locked the lock with a firm click.

Then he pocketed his skeleton key and limped behind the group, all the way into the red brick house.

When they were all inside, Cornell and Christine crawled out of the bush. They were scratchy and sweaty.

Christine unwound a grasshopper in her hair and set it on the ground.

"Cornell," Christine said. "Are you thinking what I'm thinking?"

"Yes," Cornell said.

They looked at each other and said it together.

"Zambies!"

CHAPTER EIGHT: CAPTURED!

They sat around Christine's camp stove.

Christine had brought one in her backpack. She also had a cooler full of food.

While they ate campfire stew, they talked about zambies.

"A zambie," Christine said, "is a creature that is restless until it gets what it craves. But what is it craving?"

Bob Beaton snatched the dish away.
"My candy," Bob Beaton said.
Charlie whisked the bowl away. "Mine!"

'Candy." Cornell sucked gravy off his

spoon. "They're craving candy."

"But why?" Christine asked. "Paradise Falls is full of candy."

"I don't know," Cornell said. "But I think they crave light, too."

Cornell told Christine about the old man and the bench.

"Light, hmm," Christine said. "Is that why they shut Paradise Falls down at dark?"

Cornell scraped the last of the stew into his bowl.

"Maybe," Cornell said. "But it means we can explore the house in the morning."

"Right!" Christine said. "Because they'll all go back to town."

Christine pulled out a toasting fork and stuck a marshmallow on it. "Can't go to bed hungry."

They topped chocolate squares on roasted marshmallows topped and put them between graham crackers. They are until they could eat no more.

It was now very dark. The crickets were chirping; the fireflies were flashing; and the mosquitoes were biting...Cornell.

Christine had already sprayed herself with bug spray.

"Want some bug spray, Cornell?"

Cornell slapped away another mosquito. "Sure."

He handed the bug spray back to Christine. Then Cornell fumbled in his pockets for his magic lantern.

"Madam, thank you for dinner," Cornell said. "Since we can't explore tonight, I'm going back to Seventh Heaven."

He switched on the lantern. A powerful beam lit up the path to Paradise Falls.

Christine knocked the tiny lantern to the ground.

"What's the matter with you?" she hissed. "Do you want them to run out here?"

"You broke it!"

"Be nice. Or I won't let you borrow my extra tent!"

"Extra tent?"

"Of course," Christine pulled two tents out of her backpack. "You don't think I'd be selfish and bring just one tent, do you?"

Soon Christine had two pup tents ready to go. She had put sleeping bags, pillows, and canteens in them, too.

"Sleep tight, Cornell." Christine zipped her tent closed. "Don't let the spiders bite."

Cornell zipped his tent, too, and sulked in the dark.

Cornell opened his eyes. Dawn was breaking. Robins were tweeting.

Had the zambies had left Pinecrest? Were they now at Paradise Falls?

Maybe Cornell could sneak out and do some sleuthing without Christine getting in his way.

Cornell unzipped his tent and crawled out.

Christine was standing by her tent doing jumping jacks and side bends. Cornell smelled food.

"Morning, Cornell," Christine puffed. "Got a healthy breakfast ready for you. Eat up!"

"What is it?"

"Scrambled egg whites, whole grain toast, and organic broccoli."

Christine also tossed him a book: *Creatures of the Night: Witches, Werewolves, and Vampires.*

"There's a chapter on zambies," Christine said. "I was reading about them while I made breakfast."

Cornell opened the book. He choked down the awful breakfast. But he hadn't brought any food with him. He hadn't planned for spending the night in the woods.

Some breakfast was better than no breakfast, he decided.

He read aloud to Christine as he ate.

"The book says zambies get active for the day once dawn rises out of the eastern horizon, shadows point to the west, and morning glories open their petals wide to the sun," Cornell said.

"So like eight-fifteen?" Christine said.

Cornell tossed the book to her and stretched. His stomach growled. He needed to solve the mystery and get real food.

"Jump around if you want," he said. "I have a supernatural mystery to solve."

"Go ahead," Christine huffed as she did sit-ups. "I'll catch up as soon as I reach a hundred."

Cornell took a step. "Ouch!"

He had a rock in his shoe!

So he at onto the grass and untied his shoes. By the time he got the rock out, Christine had broken down camp and slung her back backpack over her shoulder.

She was pacing, ready to go.

"Come on, Cornell," Christine said. "Hurry up so we can..."

A chorus of whoops and yells cut off her words.

"Duck," she hissed, pushing Cornell down.

The door to Pinecrest burst open. All the residents of Paradise Falls sprinted down the hill to the gate.

They were young, happy, tanned, and energetic. The warm sunshine made their lustrous hair shine and their golden tans glow with vibrant health.

They laughed, and chatted, and poked each other in fun.

And they carried things with them.

Things like beach balls.

And volleyballs.

And buckets and pails for sandcastles.

And roller skates.

And skateboards.

And swimming flippers.

The very last two in the line carried the construction cones.

Only one was old. He shuffled down

the hill with a cane. His body was bent in half.

And he was licking a giant lollipop.

"Remember," he croaked. "It's my turn to sit in the sun."

"Yeah, yeah, Delbert," they laughed.

Delbert took out his skeleton key, took off the lock, and waited for the beachcombing throngs to dash out.

Finally Delbert passed between the wrought iron fence. But then he did something very strange.

Cornell nearly gasped aloud.

Delbert propped the cane against the fence.

He popped the lollipop inside his mouth.

And then he reached inside his pocket for a giant padlock.

Delbert fastened the lock around the gate. He locked it with a key that looked like a giant doughnut.

Then Delbert picked up his cane and hobbled down the hill, licking his candy.

Christine nudged Cornell. "Ready?"

"When do they return?" Cornell asked.

"When the sun disappears below the

horizon, and the birds stop singing their daily song, and the owls and other night creatures start roaming the earth," Christine said.

"So like eight-fifteen?" Cornell asked.

Christine jabbed Cornell in the ribs. "Yep!" She jumped up. "Last one to the gate is a rotten sleuth!"

She ran off, kicking dust in his face. Cornell plodded after her. Brains were more important than speed in solving mysteries.

And Cornell had plenty of brains, he thought as he walked to the gate.

Christine was already sizing up the lock and frowning.

"Your two skeleton keys are useless, Christine," Cornell said. "Watch how a real supernatural super sleuth gets inside."

Cornell walked up and down the tall wrought iron fence. His best bet, he decided, was the large himenelac tree, about a foot away from the fence.

Like most himenelac trees, its lowest branches were about eight feet from the ground. Cornell would need his pocket stepladder to reach it.

The pocket stepladder was one of the

items Cornell deemed essential when he left Seventh Heaven on his mission. But then, he WAS the great Professor Cornell Dyer, a super supernatural sleuth.

Cornell dug in his blazer pockets until he hand closed on the tiny square wooden box. He removed the box, held it in the palm of his outstretched hands, and cried, "Sifdover, hudina, polla, OMULPORE!"

He laid the box on the ground. Instantly, it burst into a large stepladder. Cornell carried the ladder to the trees and climbed up to the branch.

After about five minutes of climbing, shimmying, and scraping his hands and knees of the himenelac's rough bark, Cornell was on the branch near the fence.

It was a long way down. But if Cornell timed it right, he could leap over the tall wrought iron and land on the other side. He'd get a few scrapes and bruises. But all super supernatural sleuthing came with risks.

Just as Cornell was about to leap, he saw a sight that sank his heart and boiled his blood.

Christine was already on the other side of the fence. She was holding up an ice cream cone key. He glanced back. The gate was open.

Christine stamped her foot. "Come, ON, Cornell! Let's go!"

Cornell climbed down the tall himenelac tree, grumbling to himself and scraping his hands and knees even more.

Then he repeated the magic words, picked up his tiny wooden box of a magic stepladder, put it back inside his blazer pocket, and joined Christine on the grounds of Pinecrest.

"A fine time you picked to go tree-climbing," Christine said. Then she saw Cornell's bleeding hands. "You're hurt. Wait."

Christine unzipped a side pouch in her backpack and pulled out a turquoise gelatin pearl.

"Magic skulking duscle," Christine said. "Chases away dirt, eats up germs, closes wounds."

"I knew that," Cornell said. "I ran out."

Christine dabbed each scrape until all the skulking duscle was absorbed.

Then they crept across the silent, shadowy yard of Pinecrest. When they reached the front door, none of their special keys worked.

Christine sighed hard. "Now what?"

"I'm thinking," Cornell said.

But thinking was too hard on an empty, growling stomach. So he reached inside his blazer pocket for a package of licorice twists.

As he chomped on one twist after another, Cornell shone his magic lantern into the lock to study its tumblers.

It looks like a licorice twist, Cornell thought.

Cornell slid a licorice twist into the lock and heard a click. He turned the handle and opened the door.

"Bravo, Cornell!" Christine exclaimed.

They stepped into the dim, gritty foyer. Then she sniffed and said, "What...what is that smell?"

Cornell sniffed, too. He wrinkled his nose.

"Musty oatmeal," he said. "Stale wheat bran." He sniffed again. "Crumbling yogurt."

The old wooden floors creaked loudly under in the airless, too-quiet building. Christine ran her finger over an old dusty buffet and started opening drawers.

Cornell wandered into the parlor. All the ornate furniture was threadbare and thick with cobwebs. The curtains were open and let in the sun.

A lone gray fish with bulging eyes swam in a large aquarium As Cornell got close, the fish flipped belly up and floated to the top.

That's when Cornell heard it.

Creak, creak, creak, creak.

He went back into the hall. Christine had stopped exploring, too. She cocked her head, listening.

Creak, creak, creak, creak.

"Cornell, what is that noi..." Christine started to say.

And then they saw it.

They saw the source of the creak.

Slowly coming down the hall toward them was a very old, very bony woman.

The woman was pushing a walker.

Her very fine, very white hair was rolled into pink rollers. She wore a faded light blue robe with faded pink carnations. She had fuzzy blue slippers on her feet.

The slippers swiffed over the floor as she rolled.

Creak, creak, creak, creak.
Swiff, swiff, swiff, swiff

Suddenly, zambies swarmed into the hall and closed around Christine.

"Cornell!" she screamed.

Before Cornell could move, they had dragged her down hall and out of sight.

CHAPTER NINE: MACABRE MUSEUM

Cornell stayed inside his motor home all day. It was a terrible, terrible day.

For one, all the wonderful Paradise Falls candy was upstairs in his room at Seventh Heaven.

Paradise Bliss candy was the sweetest, most flavorful candy he'd ever eaten. Cornell could not get enough of it.

Secondly, the zambies had Christine. If he didn't rescue her soon, would she become a zambie, too?

So while Cornell munched sugary

cereal and guzzled orange drinks, he studied up on zambies and pondered the mystery.

Was everyone in Paradise Falls zambies? How did that happen?

What about visitors? What happens to them?

Do visitors have a good time and go home? Or do they become zambies and stay forever?

Why do zambies take turns sitting in the full sun?

"Eureka!" Cornell cried.

He reached for a handful of Captain Christopher's Colorful Cereal Crunchies.

Zambies were dormant in the dark. Light kept them young during the day, Sugar gave them energy.

So Cornell would sneak back to Pinecrest at midnight, when all the zambies would be sleeping.

But he would have plenty of candy in his pockets, just in case.

He would discover its secrets and rescue Christine.

Cornell yawned and stretched out on the couch for a good long nap.

At midnight, Cornell climbed the tall himenelac tree in the dark. He vaulted over the very high wrought iron fence in the dark.

Even one beam of Cornell's magic flashlight might awaken the zambies. He could not risk it.

Instead, Cornell put on his special daylight glasses. This let him see in the darkest of dark like it was the noonest of day.

He opened the door to Pinecrest with a licorice twizzler. First stop; the parlor. Cornell wanted to check his theory.

Volleyballs, buckets and pails for sandcastles, roller skates, skateboards, swimming flippers, and orange cones were stacked in the corner, all ready for fun in the sun.

Cornell walked right to the aquarium. The gray fish with the bulging eyes was still floating on top.

So Cornell reached into his pocket. He pinched off a piece of licorice twist. Then he dropped it into the water.

Immediately the fish swam after its prize and swallowed it in one gulp.

Well done, Cornell, he told himself.

Now Cornell was ready to inspect the other rooms in Pinecrest. He wandered into the kitchen and gasped.

The kitchen was littered with old candy wrappers up to his ankle. The walls were streaked with chocolate.

But that wasn't the worse of it.

The other rooms on the first floor, the second floor, and the third floor were full of sleeping zambies, stacked one on top of the other, almost to the ceiling.

Cornell did not see Christine anywhere. But he had not looked in the basement or the attic.

He went back to the kitchen and opened the door to the basement. Cornell heard creaking and groaning, the noise old machines make when they work very, very hard.

Cornell tiptoed halfway down the stairs. He saw a very strange sight.

The basement was filled with wooden mills that looked like merry-go-rounds without the horses.

People were pushing them to make them turn. Their eyes looked blank. Their tongues hung out.

Paradise Falls candy dangled on a string in front of them.

Their eyes did not see anything but the candy.

Paradise Falls dropped out of the chutes and into giant plastic bags. The candy was wrapped and ready to eat.

Cornell turned up the magnifier on his daylight glasses for a closer look.

WHEW!

Christine was not one of those people.

He tiptoed up the stairs and then tiptoed to the third floor. At the end of the hall, he opened the attic door and climbed up the ladder.

He did not find Christine in the attic.

But he did find some answers.

The room was full newspaper clippings, framed awards, and vintage advertisements.

This is what Cornell read:

Confit's Confectionary wins 'best chocolate' again!

Best cotton candy at 1919 state fair goes to Confit's Confectionary.

No sweet is as delightful as Confit's Confectionary.

A bonbon by Confit's Confectionary is better than day in the sun.

For the energy rush that lasts – choose Confit's Confectionary.

Fire destroys famous Confit Confectionary sugar cane fields.

Will Confit's Confectionary rise again?

A strong hand clamped around Cornell's neck.

A gruff voice said, "What do you think you're doing?"

Cornell broke free of the grasp and whirled around.

It was Christine, grinning.

CHAPTER TEN: A SUGAR HIGH THAT MUSTN'T DIE

"You!" Cornell whispered. "Are you a..."

"Zambie?" Christine tossed her head. "No, silly. They didn't want me. They only wanted the candy in my backpack."

"Then why are you still here?"

"Because I was sleuthing." Christine tugged his hand. "Come see what I found."

Christine led Cornell to the back of the attic. A young, tanned blonde girl in shorts and a halter top sat in the corner. The girl was crying.

"This is Amanda," Christine said. "She is the oldest zambie. She's the leader. She's the only zambie that gets to eat candy all day and all night. Please give her a chocolate bar."

"Why should I?" Cornell said.

"She won't talk unless she has sugar," Christine said. "I've already given her all of mine."

"Who cares?" Cornell said. "I've solved the mystery. Pinecrest is really an old candy factory. The candy factory is run by zambies. And the zambies run Paradise Falls. They live on sugar and sunlight. They're harmless."

"They're in trouble," Christine said. "And they're not harmless. If they don't get enough sugar, they'll eat people for their blood sugar."

Cornell rolled his eyes.

"Tell him, Amanda," Christine said.

Amanda shook her head. "I want sugar first."

Cornell sighed loudly. Then he pulled out a chocolate bar and gave it to Amanda. She gobbled it in three bites.

"We keep running out of sugar," Amanda said.

"Impossible!" Cornell exclaimed. "Paradise Falls is full of sugar."

"It's not enough for all the zambies."

"Madam, explain," Cornell said, irritably.

"More candy," Amanda said.

Cornell sighed loudly again. "Then he pulled out a giant orange sucker and gave it to Amanda. She tore off the wrapper and ate it in three bites.

"We created Paradise Falls because we need people to make our candy," Amanda said. "The zambies will starve without sugar."

"Why can't they just buy more sugar?" Cornell asked.

"We do buy more sugar," Amanda said.

"Then what's the problem?" Cornell asked.

"Candy," Amanda said.

Cornell peeled off three licorice twists and gave them to Amanda. She ate them in three bites.

"My family owned Confit Confectionary. To make our candy, we grew a special sugar cane," Amanda said. "They grew many, many fields of it. No one in the whole world grew it. That's why our candy tasted so good. Everyone wanted our candy.

Everyone bought our candy."

"Keep going," Cornell said.

"Candy!" Amanda said.

"Nope."

Amanda began to cry.

Cornell sighed loudly. He peeled off three more licorice twists. She ate them in three bites.

"One night a mean person set our fields on fire," Amanda said. "It made a lot of sugar cane smoke. But it wasn't regular sugar cane smoke. All our workers breathed the smoke. I was one of those workers. That smoke altered our air forever. It changed us into zambies. We will dry up without light. We will die without sugar."

Christine turned to Cornell. "Don't you see? People who come to Paradise Falls have so much fun, they want to stay forever. The candy tastes so good, they want to help make it. But when people stay too long, they become zambies."

"We've used up all our sugar," Amanda said. "So we buy more and more. But we end up with more and more zambies. We can't keep up."

Christine took Amanda's hand. "It's

wrong to trick people into making your candy."

"But we'll starve!"

"You won't starve," Cornell said. "And you won't have to eat people for their blood sugar. I have an idea."

Christine gasped and clutched his arm. "Are you thinking what I'm thinking?"

"Maybe," Cornell said.

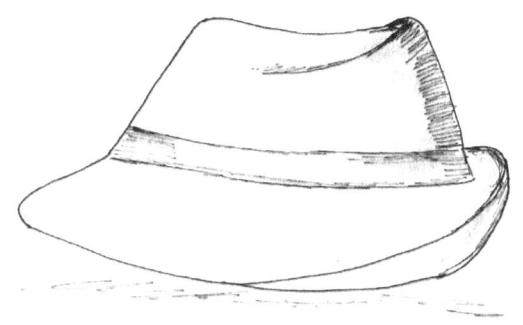

EPILOGUE

Cornell explained his plan to Amanda. The zambies could hire a factory to make plenty of their special candy. They could pay for the candy with money they earned at the shops at Paradise Falls.

"I know just the place," Christine said. "I exorcised a poltergeist from a candy factory in Oklahoma last year. These factory workers will understand. They will gladly make your candy for you."

"Then you can let visitors stay at Paradise Falls a short time and then go home," Cornell said. "People will be sorry to leave and happy to come back. Then Paradise Falls will keep earning money for their candy."

Christine nodded. "And no one else will turn into zambies."

"But you'll need to reopen all the bricked-up rooms in your inns," Cornell said. "This way, more people can come to Paradise Falls for rest and fun."

Amanda thought about Cornell's words. "That sounds like a good plan. But it won't work."

"Why not?" Cornell said.

"Because we're almost out of candy. We need candy made right away."

Christine laughed. "I can fix that."

As it turns out, Christine had many big boxes of candy jewelry in her motor home.

"The candy factory gave it to me," Christine said. "They were so happy the poltergeist was gone. But it's too much for me to eat by myself. You can eat this candy while you wait for the factory to make more of your candy."

When the sun came up, the young and strong zambies happily carried all the boxes of candy jewelry out of Christine's motor home and into Pinecrest.

After that, Cornell and Christine decided to leave before they became zambies. They had both stayed at Paradise Falls a long time.

"I hope you come back soon," Amanda said. She had looped three candy necklaces around her neck and three candy necklaces on each wrist.

"I had a great time," Cornell said. "I can't wait to book another vacation here."

"Don't forget to call the factory," Christine said.

"We won't," Amanda said. She picked up the last box from Christine's motor home and walked away.

"Well done, Professor," Christine grabbed Cornell's hand and shook it "We make a great team."

"Maybe we should work toget…"

"The world is full of supernatural mysteries," Christine said. "It's good that two supernatural super sleuths are out there solving them. One is not enough."

"True," Cornell reluctantly agreed.

"So we should get going."

Christine climbed into her motor home and shut the door. She started up the motor. Then she turned to Cornell, touched the brim of her hat, and grinned.

"See ya 'round, partner," she said.

Then Christine drove away.

Cornell hurried to his motor home. He was eager to leave, too. Become a zambie? Cornell shuddered. He had many mysteries to solve.

He decided to take a different road out of Paradise Falls. This road led past the back of Pinecrest and to the highway.

Cornell switched on the radio and found his favorite Wagnerian opera. The sun was shining. A warm breeze through the open window. It was a good day for adventures.

But as Cornell passed Pinecrest, the music began to fade and crackle. And then he saw two sights that worried him.

Yes, Cornell thought. He would return one day.

But not for a vacation.

This is what he saw.

Most of the candy jewelry boxes were already empty and stacked up behind the house.

That was the first sight.

The second sight was just as bad.

Zambies crowded the windows at Pinecrest. They watched Cornell drive past.

The zambies were biting their candy jewelry. Most of them had bitten away most of the candy. A few were chewing the string.

By the time Cornell reached the highway, the radio had stopped crackling and was playing opera music.

He was also ready for lunch. He'd shared a box of doughnuts with Christine when the zambies came for the boxes. But that was all. He was starving.

Food, Cornell thought, reading the signs along the road.

Then Cornell's motor home phone rang. He answered it with his mind because it's not safe to touch anything except the steering wheel when one is driving.

"This is The Thaumaturgical World of Professor Cornell Dyer: I specialize in Amulets, Fortune-Telling (with and without cards), Ghost-Hunting, Horoscopes, Numerology, Palm-Reading, Potions, Séances, Spells, and Vampire-Slaying. How may I help you?"

"Professor Dyer!" the woman scolded

him. "When are you getting rid of the haunted lake in my back yard!"

"I'll be right there," Cornell said. "Just as soon as I have lunch and cross a few state lines."

SYMBOLISM

Companies that made candy, sugar, and other products with sugar used to say sugar helped gave people, especially children, lots of energy.

There is some science behind this. When people eat, food is broken down into glucose. This is a type of sugar. The body uses this sugar for energy. If a person's body gets too low on glucose, the person might feel tired or shaky. The person might even faint. A small piece of candy can quickly raise the glucose in the person's blood.

But too much sugar is not good for a person's health or teeth. A well-balanced diet will keep the right amount of glucose in the body.

Some years later, scientists decided sugar can make some children become overactive or hyperactive. Many scientists don't believe it anymore.

People used to think lots of time in the sun gave a healthy tan. But research shows too much sun can hurt the skin.

Sugar cane is a tall perennial grass

that's used to make sugar. A perennial plant lives two years or more.

"White Zombies" is the name of a 1932 movie. Many zombie movies created their zombies based on this one. In this movie, an evil voodoo master uses zombies to run his sugar mill.

The way Cornell and Christine estimate time near Pinecrest is a parody of several scenes from the 2015-2017 television series "Galavant."

About the Author

Denise M. Baran-Unland is the author of the BryonySeries supernatural/literary trilogy for young and new adults, the Adventures of Cornell Dyer chapter book series for grade school children and the Bertrand the Mouse series for young children.

She has six adult children, three adult stepchildren, fourteen total grandchildren, six godchildren, and four cats.

She is the co-founder of WriteOn Joliet and previously taught features writing for a homeschool coop, with the students' work published in the co-op magazine and The Herald-News in Joliet.

Denise blogs daily and is currently the features editor at The Herald-News. To read her feature stories, visit www.theherald-news.com. For more information about Denise's fiction and to follow her on social media, visit www.bryonyseries.com.

Sue Midlock lives in Illinois with her husband and has been writing for 10 years. She started writing when the book "Twilight" first came out and fell in love with the paranormal genre.

Since then, she has written and finished her Rosewood Trilogy and just recently her anniversary edition, "Forever," which is the first book re-written for adults.

Her most recent releases are "Southern Shorts," which is an anthology of short stories about Dry Prong, Louisana and "Night Games."

Timothy Baran enjoys cooking on professional and home levels. He also likes writing dark poetry and stories whose style mimics C. S. Lewis, his favorite author.

He is currently working on his first novel and a book of poetry.

But he especially loves his cat Midnight, whom he raised from a kitten.